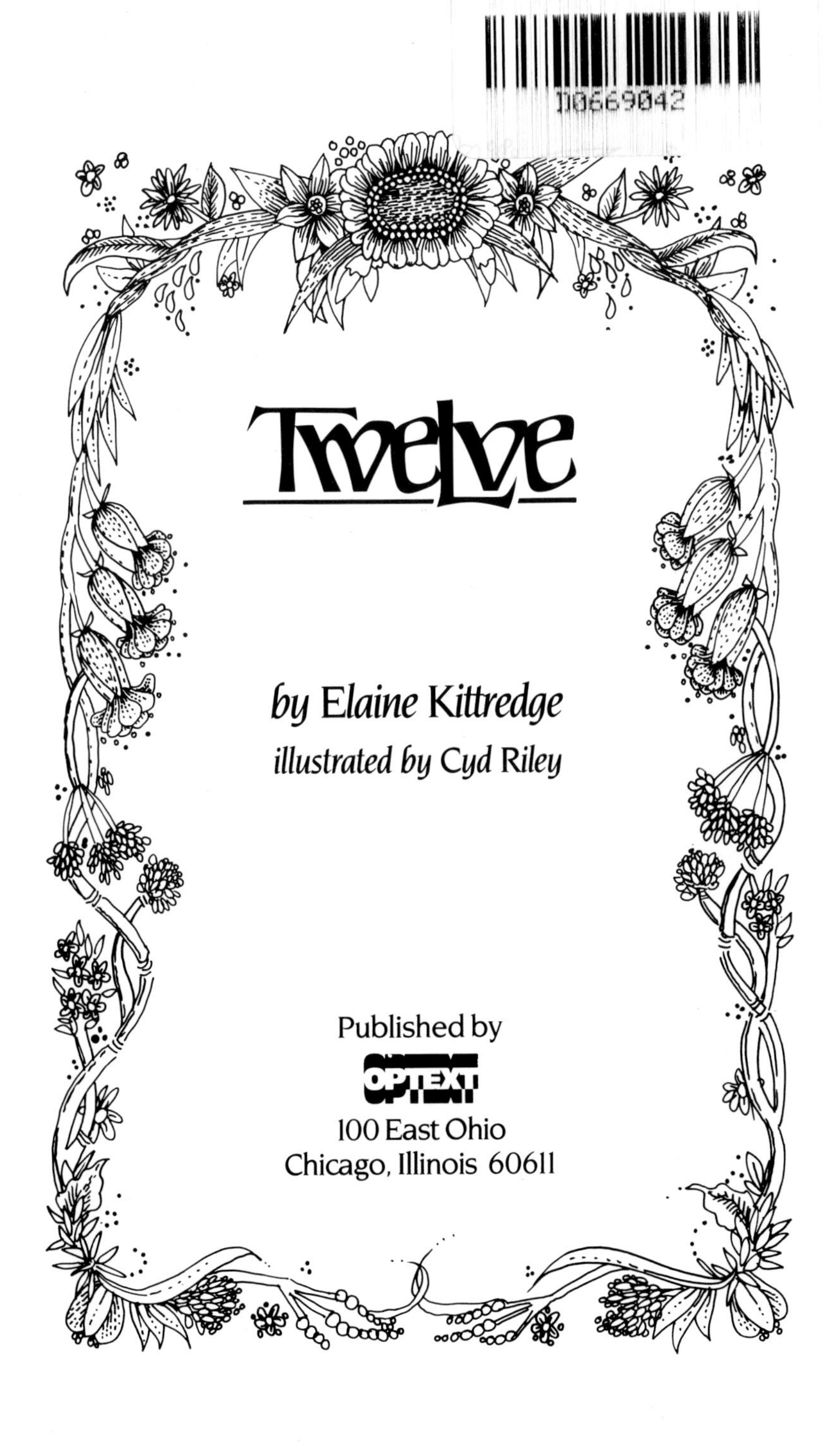

Twelve

by Elaine Kittredge

illustrated by Cyd Riley

Published by

OPTEXT

100 East Ohio

Chicago, Illinois 60611

Published by:

100 East Ohio
Chicago, Illinois 60611

ISBN 0-9611266-1-2

fourth printing

To My Friend, The Tree Who Lives on the Corner of Magnolia & Victoria, Chicago, Illinois

I stand here, a tree
next to the mailbox
unnoticed by passersby.
But the wee nature spirits
of the neighborhood
are attuned to my spirit.
Each sunset caresses me.
Each sunrise I grow a bit.
And the wind plays with my leaves
(sometimes a little bit rough).
The birds of the neighborhood
sleep in the privacy of my shadows
and sing with vibrant rapture
every morning.
Insects of all variety feed from
my small, hidden baskets of treasure
which mankind foolishly views as waste.
I am long-lived and patient.
I silently bless those who pass
and protect those who live
in the houses and buildings that I shade.
My view is farther reaching than my needs.
And the gift of "tree" is as sacred
to God's loving eye as the gift of "man".

Preface

TWELVE *is for kids, but it's also one of those children's books for adults.* For *the kid with a big people's body, who tends to get wrapped up in responsibilities and sometimes forgets there's a hot flame of creativity and wonder inside.*

I *called it "Twelve" for several reasons. Twelve seems to be a mystical number related to change and transformation.* It *is also the threshold of a child's life when he can still relate to childhood, yet senses the changes he will treasure as an adult.*

I *wanted* TWELVE *to be a joyous inner adventure story.* I *hope it is, and that it opens and reopens hearts and spiritual doors that are just waiting to be entered.*

In real life Jimmy *isn't necessarily a little boy.* He *is a little person.* Gramatically I *say "he" but* I *mean he/she.* Reading *he/she is distracting to me.* I *was glad to be a little girl, as* I *am to be a woman.* I *really believe we're all the same inside, and this book is about the inside.* I *start the book in the first person before changing to the third, so you realize that you are* Jimmy.

The tree is real. It's a beautiful, old Linden *tree on the corner of* Magnolia *and* Victoria *in* Chicago. I *never sat under it, but* I *did hug it when* I *was sure no one would see me and think* I *was crazy.*

This preface is only for adults. Neither *kids nor adults enjoy prefaces; however, short ones are tolerable to adults.*

Thanks to all who helped TWELVE *become a reality.*

1

I woke up suddenly. I thought my bed fell through a hole in the sky, but all was quiet except for a few cars.

I pulled the comforter over my head, then pushed it away because I couldn't breathe. One of those things I always forget.

I lay there a long time watching the moonshadows slide over my bed. It must be special to lie in the moonlight, so I moved my body as the light moved, and must have fallen asleep. I don't know. At least I hope I fell asleep, because I heard music far away and felt as though I were floating. It felt so good floating around, I decided not to be afraid. I don't remember much more than this.

The next day was like any other day, except I kept wondering about floating around in my dreams.

That night I went to bed with some questions. The rules were broken. People are supposed to stay on the ground, not float all over.

As my water bed sloshed to an even keel, I closed my eyes, but didn't sleep. I was wide awake. My body felt heavy. Then heavier, heavier. Down, down I went. Deeper and deeper. Darker and darker. It felt as though

I were sliding down a long banister. I didn't know where I was going — but *liked* it. Colors appeared, then disappeared: dark purple; blue with sudden flashes of white lightning. I slid downward, then became weightless. With the air I began floating toward the stars. Then I could see and feel the black night as though it were my skin. Suddenly I shot upward, faster and faster. I started swimming through the air, weightlessly turning slow summersaults.

All through the dream I wondered where I was because it was so real. It felt like more than a little dream. This was a big one.

Chapter 2

The next night I had more strange dreams. For some reason they did not frighten me. I remember hearing: "Hey, kid! What's your name?"

Everything became clear—the lines in the drapes, the edge of the bed. Nothing was fuzzy like a typical dream. There was an elf standing on my windowsill.

"Jimmy...my name is Jimmy. Actually, it's James. But little kids have to be called 'Jimmy.' My friends would laugh at me if they called me 'James.'"

"So, then, you have two names."

"No. I have a big name and a little name. When I'm big, they'll call me 'James.'"

"What is big? This is a bit confusing for me."

"When I get a job, I guess."

"You look pretty big to me, Jimmy. And what's a *job*?"

I looked at him. He was two feet tall. I *must* have been "pretty big" to him. And I didn't really know what a *job* was. His bright, happy eyes and bushy brows were etched with golden flickers. The dancing light reminded me of sparklers my dad bought for July 4th. He moved his arms with excitement as he spoke. What I noticed most was how happy he was. His laughter affected even the air around us. His shoes turned up at the ends, and he could have blended in easily with the plants because of his green and brown clothing.

"Jimmy, you're right. I do live with the plants."

"Holy cow! He knows what I'm thinking!", Jimmy thought, quite silently.

"Of course I know! There are *many* ways to talk. Sometimes words don't work well enough. What if you need to tell someone a lot very quickly — in a time of danger, for instance. You must first focus all your thoughts into one dot and shoot it at them. They pick it up and translate it instantly. Silently. No one knows but you two. And what about long distances? Oh, yes, we really need thought *tones* as much as we need words."

"I never thought of it that way. Will you teach me how to do it?"

"Sure, Jimmy. But no one can *really* teach you anything but yourself. And you have to practice. Nothing comes easily. And there are no guarantees."

The summer breeze blew the drapes. They came alive in the night's moonlight. Swishing. Swishing. And then he was gone. Elf? Faerie? Would he ever come back? I can't even call him because I don't know his name. Unless... "Why of course! That's what he told me: to focus all my thoughts into a point and shoot it to him. Yes. That's what I'll do." My consciousness rode the swishing drapes into a deep, heavy slumber.

3

The morning came with the rustle of wind, and rays of sunshine flooded the bedroom. I watched the sunlight creep across the floor until it reached the dresser. Then I thought about school—how out of place I felt there. I truly wished that my teacher were "real" like my mom. Real people were so nice to be around. I can talk to my mom, laugh with her, and even cry on her shoulder. She never tells me to stop, or that "it could be worse", or some other nonsense. She just listens and holds me. I can even get really *mad* at her, and somehow she always knows exactly what I mean, even if I say it wrong. Yep. I felt rather lucky about getting her. But my *teacher*, now *she* was another story. Old "Beanbag" Biedermann never knows what I mean, even when I say it *right*! She always looks for mistakes and is overjoyed when she finds them. What a mean person! Even her shoes are horrid. Oh, well, she must have some good points, somewhere.

I rolled over and hugged my pillow. The scent of moss and cool grass slid past my nose. A vacation passed over by two years still existed somewhere. Otherwise, how could I smell it now? Jody had taken me to Washington State and I still could envision the waterfalls and forests. The mystery and delight of ancient

trees always fascinated me. That's when I first started to believe in other creatures. The Indians knew about life — tree spirits, wind spirits. And the Irish — *they* believe in elves and faeries, little people made of the spirit and wind, sunlight and God.

I stumbled to my sock drawer, found two that *sort* of matched and went back to sit on the edge of a chair — as well as I could with all the clothes I had to balance on. "Why don't I live in a place that *believes*?" I looked into the face of my big toe. No answer. I wiggled it, stopped, wiggled it again in reply and then covered it with a sock.

My mother knocked on the door.

"You up, hon?"

"Yeah, mom."

"Would you like some breakfast?"

"Maybe just some toast."

"Okay. Want jelly?"

"No."

She came in to greet me. As she moved gracefully, putting a few books into their proper slots on the shelf, I watched her and felt warm surges of love come from deep inside my heart.

"Hey, mom. Do you believe in elves and faeries?" I didn't really think she'd say *yes*, but at least I could share a little of what was happening to me.

She thought seriously for several moments. "I didn't *use* to think about it. I know the Celts believed in them. At times I think there is more to life than meets the eye..."

"Well, do you *believe* in them?"

My mother sat down. "There's a place I read about not too long ago—I think it's in England or Scotland—called Findhorn. People who started the community are very sure that each type of plant and tree has its own special plant spirit. They call them "devas." And the people who live there have been able to grow beautiful, large flowers, vegetables and trees on a cold, infertile beach. Things that are not made to grow in that climate. I don't doubt it a bit, although I don't quite understand it either. Since I've read that book I've been longing to take a trip to see it for myself. Maybe even take a freighter so I can have a lot of time to sit and think and watch the sun come up over the ocean..." Her voice trailed off as she gazed dreamily out of the window. All of a sudden she popped back to the bedroom.

"Would you find the book for me, mom? I'd really like to read it if it isn't too hard."

"Sure, Jimmy. Today. Remind me when I get home from work and I'll find it."

"You're all right, mom."

"I love you too, Jimmy. I'm really glad you picked me."

I finished getting dressed. Somehow I lost my resentment for the Old Beanbag, and now all I could think about was the book. Maybe OB Biedermann has a first name. I'm sure her mother didn't call her OB Biedermann or Beanbag. She might even have been little once. Maybe even nice.

Chapter 4

On my way to school I *knew* there was something more. More. More than I was seeing. More than I was hearing. More than I was letting in. The grass was still wet, and I sat down by a big round tree trunk. I wanted to sit there and feel it on my back. I didn't want to go to school. I didn't want to see The Biedermann. I knew I would end up staring out of the window, because that's what I always ended up doing every day after the first half hour.

I made a bargain with myself. I would go to school, but I would be late. Warm sunrays danced between leaves and made shadows on my eyelids, and I *think* I started to sleep. Something was happening that was like thinking, yet not quite, because instead of thinking words, I thought whole paragraphs at a time, even pages—but there were no words.

I don't know how long I stayed there. The left side of my face was warm. Then I started to dream. Yet it wasn't exactly a *dream*.

The tree was moving gently behind my back. I could feel the water seeping up slightly underneath the bark. The bark felt like the skin of a big quiet animal. It seemed more alive than before, almost as though it were breathing. I sat there for a long time feeling the

tree. Were all trees alive like this, and we only make too much noise and move too fast to notice? I had taken trees for granted, almost as though they were alive for me instead of for themselves, too.

I blanked out of this reality and entered a strange environment. It seemed as though the tree had pulled me onto its back and we were trudging through a dark, dense forest. The smells of moss and rain came back. We moved forward steadily. I knew we were going to a very important place, not scary, exactly, but *really* important. The closer we got, the deeper the meaning felt. Deeper, deeper, and deeper yet. Noise hurt my ears. It was a noise I didn't *hear.* It was a noise I *felt* deep inside the center of my brain.

Then it reached a screeching pitch and everything suddenly became silent. Absolutely silent.

"Jimmy!"

"Yes, I'm Jimmy."

"You have been chosen to be a tree and plant friend. Your job is to find a way to bring humans back to tree entities so that we may share our wisdom and love of the planet. We don't have a lot of time, Jimmy. Can you work with us?"

"I don't know what I can do. How many people believe that trees are more than things to fill the parkways or parks, or for climbing, or burning in a fireplace?"

"Jimmy, that's your job. We believe you can do it."

"Holy cow! I'm just a KID! What do I know about things like that?"

"Jimmy, a kid is a *little* people, not a *stupid* people... And besides that, we intend to help you carry this out. It's very important. Very important indeed, and we feel you are sensitive enough to be helpful to the planet and its friends."

The sunlight blazed into my eyes. I woke up startled by a squirrel jumping past my arm. I ran all the way to school terrified. Tree entities. Where had I gone in those short moments? Was I crazy? Worse. Who could I tell?

5

All day was like a dream. Each noise had an echo. Every eye was looking at me. I heard voices laughing.

"What's wrong with you, Jimmy? You're really strange today!" Ms. Biedermann remarked coldly.

My friends avoided me. Each time I would walk up to a group, they seemed to stop talking, then looked at me strangely. What agony this was. What terrible and hurting agony. What was I doing to cause such awful attention? Why didn't they just do what they always did?

Each time my thoughts strayed, I fell back into a fantasy of trees talking. I knew something important had happened, yet it scared me.

School finally ended for the day. My face was stuck in a book. Everyone left the room and at last it was silent. I sat alone at my desk running a pencil up a crack in the wood. The desk—*that* was once a tree. No bugs or birds in it now, just old lunch bags and books. A few crayons. One paper clip. Crumbs.

I got up and walked to the window. Overlooking the soccer field were bleachers and trees. Trees. Was everything made out of trees? My books, the paper I wrote on, the pencils I wrote with, the floors I walked on, my lunchbags...everything seemed to be made out of trees.

I turned toward the door. The janitor was mopping the halls and already the sun was casting long shadows on the streaked floor. I put my things together and fit them carefully into my backpack.

The sun followed me home. I don't remember the walk, just my shadow leaping the sidewalk cracks. My feet kept a steady rhythm with the sidewalk sections. One, two, line—one, two, line. I crossed the street then stopped cold. There in front of me was the tree I had sat by the long morning. The morning seemed so far away, as though a week had passed. Cautiously I stepped closer, then put my forehead against the bark. I started to cry. And I cried hard. I sat down against the tree, once more, but this time because I was too embarrassed to go home with my face all blotchy and tear-stained.

I thought, "A few minutes. I'll sit here for just a little bit." Oh, how good this felt. My fear left after I sat for a long while. Suddenly I realized it must be late, so I picked up my backpack, slung it over my shoulders, and headed toward home, my longshadow leading the way. I felt better now. My fears had dissolved with my tears. Funny that *tears* rhymes with *fears*.

This was from
Jimmy's
point of view—
Now,
the story goes on,
but from
another's view—
the view of his
"unseen guardian."

Chapter 6

Jimmy knew he wasn't crazy. He knew, yet he wasn't sure. None of his friends talked about things of this nature. He didn't dare talk *crazy* or they would tease him unmercifully. They already gave him a hard time, and this would only make things worse.

When he got home, as his mother promised, the book he would learn to treasure was lying on his bed.

Jimmy read every spare moment he could—on the bus, when he got home from school, and in the very early morning, at times even before the sun woke up. Sometimes the adults got very complicated, using too many words to say what they meant. Or they got preachy sounding. But at other times, he was so completely entranced by the book, he himself was talking to the faeries. They, too, he believed, are just as real as people. But people's eyes could see only in black and white, compared to *real* eyes that could see in color. Those eyes could see the faeries—*that* he knew for certain. Yet he knew *those* eyes grew from the inside out—so he had to make them grow with his thoughts.

Often he resisted going to school. He would carefully lay his book next to his leaf collection (only leaves that had fallen).

One morning as he was tying his shoes, he remembered how he had labored tying shoes when he was a little boy. Perhaps, in a year or so, he could look back and wonder why believing in faeries and elves had been so difficult. Adults believed in *angels*. At least they said they did. They believed in God too, or some special force, and God had to be a lot more difficult to understand than faeries. And faeries were beautiful and happy creatures, made to water the plants and flowers with faerie dust and love. More worthy of belief than a creepy old devil. He knew his friends would laugh, so he shared these treasured thoughts only with his mother. At least for a while.

It was quiet in the apartment. Occasionally children walked by talking and laughing on their way home from school. He could hear the birds, and cars would go by with their mechanical rattles intermixing with nature quite unconcerned. City noises filled the air, which wafted through the windows in breezy swirls.

Jimmy was propped up on pillows scrunched into the soft carpet. Almost immediately he was in the forest, and it was nearing nightfall. The insects were singing. He was scared—the kind of scared that means mystery rather than evil. Soon there was no outside light, but rather a greenish glow, like the air lighting itself. He walked farther into the denseness knowing the outside world—the world in which he was so familiar—was far behind him now. The branches and vines opened before his feet to make the path easier to tread. He knew he was there for a purpose.

His eyes focused on a clearing flooded with sunlight. There were smooth boulders and rocks, so he hoisted himself up and lay flat with his chin on his arm. The warmth of the boulder felt good under his stomach. He was there to wait. And wait he would, until whatever was supposed to happen happened.

Jimmy sensed an object to his left. Out of the corner of his eye he saw movement—but so slight. He stopped breathing to hear better. Nothing. Soon he heard a low voice.

"Why are you here? This is a sacred grove of the faeries of this wood. I assume you are friendly. You are still a child."

I'm here because I want to know some faeries. But my eyes can't see you. It only looks like a flutter out of the *side* of my eye. I want to learn how to *see* you."

"That is not so easy, because we are made of lighter material, and your eyes are accustomed to seeing only heaviness."

"Can I learn how to see lightness?"

"That kind of vision is learned from the heart. It's an act of love."

"What should I do to develop that kind of vision?"

"You can see out of every part of your body, not just your eyes. You can see with your hands, you can see with the back of your neck. And the finest vision of all is seeing with your heart."

"I think I understand that. It's like loving someone. It changes how you see them."

"Yes. I'll help you learn this vision if you wish. When

the time is right, at different moments in your life, I will show you how to see. And you may come back here whenever you wish. I must leave you now."

Jimmy felt the air change, and then he felt alone. He jumped from the boulder, patted it goodbye, then headed into the forest on his way back to the other world. Again the vines and branches parted. He tried to look at them with his heart. It was a nice feeling.

If it was a nap, he liked his dream. If it was not a nap, he liked his reality.

Chapter 7

A lot of things were happening in Jimmy's life right now. His dad had died a year ago. That was tough. But now the pain was easing and he could cope with the real world again. Whatever that was. He was still behind in renewing his friendships. Kids don't seem to wait around when there's something to do, and they all shrank away, as though contact with Jimmy would make their own dad die. So little by little his life was getting back to normal. He had one or two friends, and he was doing fairly well at school. He liked his mom and her friends, who hugged him a lot and joked with him. He especially treasured his mom because she wasn't like all the other moms. She hollered sometimes when she was frustrated. But she never made him feel like packing his bags. She laughed a lot and treated him important. Not because she had to, but because he *was* important. That felt good.

She went out a lot and "played" — as she called it. Playing almost always involved laughing and happiness, so he knew it was okay. A lot of times she took him along, and he saw new people and did new things. His albums and tapes became alive when he could go to concerts. And all her friends loved him dearly. Most of all her friend Joel.

Joel was mom's special friend. He loved her in a way that the faerie said—he saw her with his heart. The evenings they all spent together were joyful. Each time got better.

One Saturday Joel and Jimmy were cleaning the basement. It was fun rummaging through baby toys and things deciding what to keep and what to give away. That day Joel said he'd like it if Jimmy would adopt him and call him "Dad". It was a tough one to feel—he felt all choked up inside. It was not a tough question to answer. So now, as his mom had adopted Jimmy at birth, Jimmy now adopted Joel. In fact the three of them had adopted themselves right into a family. From then on Joel was his Dad. It was okay when Joel came to stay. He unpacked his bags with Jimmy's help. Again Jimmy was seeing with his heart.

The longer Joel lived with them, the closer Jimmy felt toward him. When Jimmy had more courage, he said, "You know, I've been thinking a lot about plants and trees. I think they are more alive than people give them credit for. I even believe they can talk to you—without words." This last he said with a bit of blunderbust—it seemed to sound so outrageous. He was a bit surprised with the answer.

"I agree with you, Jim. I think plants have a consciousness just like people. Well, not *just* like people; but the same kind of thing, only much less obvious. I believe rocks have awareness, too. Have you ever sat on a rock and you knew *it* knew you were there? Rocks have been around a *long* time. They probably have been through a number of earth changes. Most of the boulders in the Southwest were once at the bottom of an ocean. So, in a way, they have a lot of 'earth wisdom' wrapped up in their tough hides."

Well, that was a real surprise. An adult who thought about rocks. He sure picked a good one to adopt. At least one other large human had a sense of imagination.

"No kidding? You mean you really *believe* that?"

"Sure I do. And I've thought about it a long time. But I don't always think with my head, you know."

Jimmy flashed on the faerie and remembered his talk about seeing with all parts of the body. He wondered if perhaps one also could *think* with all parts of one's body.

"How can you think with something other than your head?"

"Most people don't know how. But it's very basic. When is the last time you stepped on a piece of jagged concrete on your way to school?"

"I only did that *once,*" Jimmy winced.

"You bet. You only needed once. Next time you passed the same spot I bet you didn't do it again."

"Well...so? What does that mean?"

"Do you think your *foot* remembered or your *brain*?"

"Wow! I guess my *foot* remembered. My foot was what got *hurt,* too."

Jimmy thought about that for many days. Seeing with your heart and thinking with your foot. Some turn that was.

Chapter 8

Jimmy went to bed that night filled with wonder. As he turned off the light he wished for a dream to help him learn more about plants and rocks. He fell asleep with Findhorn and a fallen leaf bookmark adrift on his pajamas. His mother sensed his slumber and quietly quenched the light.

He drifted deeply into the black substance of sleep. Lower, farther away. Into another universe system not unlike our own in many ways. Jimmy's body was heavily asleep, but his mind was acutely awake and aware of his surroundings. He was near the end of the tunnel now, and he could see light. Traveling backwards, on his back, headfirst, he slid into the light at last. The green countryside was like Oz, a rich and alive emerald green.

His back rested against a tree now, but such a tree as he'd never before seen. Its trunk must have been three feet in diameter. He was still getting used to things here, and decided to talk with the tree if he could.

"What kind of a tree are you?"

"What kind of question is that?"

"A normal question, I guess."

"I must be a normal tree, then, I guess."

"Well I've never seen a tree like *you* before."

"Ditto. I've never seen a tree like *you* before, either."

"I'm not a tree."

"Well, fancy that."

"You *gotta be* kidding. You know I'm not a tree. I'm a BOY."

"Oh. What is a boy? I don't know any boys."

"Boys are the opposite sex as girls."

"Well, then, what is a *girl*? And what is a *sex*?"

"Oh for heaven's sake!"

"Yes, of course, I know what a heaven is. I'm familiar with that. Because this is heaven where my roots are, and where my branches reach."

"How can heaven be where your roots are?"

"Because where your roots are, that also is where your heaven should be. Or your hell, as the case may be."

"You don't make any sense at all."

"Why should I? That is not a criterion. Not for me it isn't. I'm a TREE."

"Oh, I don't *believe* this. Why are you such an ornery tree?"

"That's a judgment. There are no judgments in heaven. Only in hell. So you must be from hell."

"I am NOT FROM HELL! I'm from EARTH!"

"Oh? How do you define *earth*?"

"It has rivers and streams and mountains and lakes. It has land with trees and bushes and flowers. It has children and big people, and dogs and birds and cats."

"What a funny place to live."

"It isn't funny at all."

"That's too bad. It must be hell."

"You make me want to scream! You don't understand *anything*. I think even my worst friend is smarter than YOU!!!"

"Oh my. Your face is quite red. Please do sit down. I certainly didn't mean to upset you. In fact I like you — even though you are rather impetuous."

Jimmy sat down and cried. He cried and he cried and he cried. His mother came into the room and put her hand on his back until he started to breathe normally. Then she tiptoed out quietly.

"I'm very sorry I offended you. I was actually playing. But I have to admit, I really don't understand what you said. It is very foreign to me."

Jimmy started seeing with his heart again. He finally pulled himself to full height and said, "I wish to come back another time and discuss this." With that, he slid into his transport tunnel and returned to his earthly bed. Heaven or hell, it sure felt good to him.

9

Crunchy toast in one world. Talking trees in another world. How many worlds are there, anyhow? How much can a ten-year-old kid handle?

Maybe the best thing about the other world he was finding was that it made the everyday world so much better. Every color seemed brighter, and every person seemed to take on his own special glow. Soon Jimmy found himself making friends with people who used to avoid him. Maybe he had been avoiding them. The more he talked to them, the more they talked to him. It didn't have to be important. All of a sudden what was important got mixed up—everything was just as important as everything else. And nothing was important enough to make you feel bad, because then you were looking at it the wrong way. His life became easier and much happier. He laughed a lot now. When he laughed he felt really good, right down to his toes. He started to run sometimes instead of walk, when he wasn't in a hurry. He found himself waking up earlier. In the mornings he could go into the back yard and feel the wet grass under his feet and look across the fence at Tom's garden.

Sometimes there were questions. Big questions. Not like a quiz. But BIG questions. Like why did his dad die? Why did anyone have to die? What was dying? And why was everybody so scared of dying? What happened after that? Did you have to look at the ground in the dark forever? Did you float on a cloud? Did you burn up or have horrid things crawl on you? What is all this "death" stuff?

That night when Jimmy went to bed, he decided to focus his dream stuff on the death stuff. Often when he dreamed, things were answered, not with a spoken voice, but answered in a quiet way. So he kissed Joel goodnight, kissed his mom goodnight, made sure the guinea pigs were fed, and slipped beneath the sheets under his soft brown comforter.

He had learned to put his body to sleep.

Why is that unusual?

Because his mind stayed awake.

Yet he slept the sleep of angels.

His mind was alert as a fox. As a panther. As a mountain lion over her cubs. And as awake as Jimmy had ever been in his life. That was when his teachers came to him. Not school teachers but dream teachers. And they laughed. Not like Ms. Biedermann. She never laughed. Maybe that's why he never listened to her too seriously. He distrusted people who didn't laugh. There seemed to be a major flaw in sorts like that. But these teachers were his *real* teachers. What they said was so unusual, but always felt right. Felt good. Not necessarily what he wanted to hear all the time. And maybe that's why he was so sure they were his teachers.

This night they told him:

"Do not concern yourself with death. That is not important. Tonight we want to talk about colors. Yellow, blue, green—these colors are like music. Color is one of the essences of life. Color is pure. Life is pure. And when we say pure we don't mean without sin. You know the real meaning of the word sin? It means 'off the mark'. You miss the bull's eye. The bull's eye is the goal, and when you miss it, you are simply off the mark. It doesn't mean *bad*. Or that you will burn in a proverbial "hell"—it means, simply, *off the mark*. Color is an essence of purity. An essence of joy. The reality of reality. Color can heal; color can soothe you. Color is your mood. What color would you use for your mood now? Pink? Yellow? Green? Blue? Which shade? You see—it is not *too* simple. There are very important differences."

Chapter 10

Summer was over. School had begun.

In the morning the sun peeked around the curtain. When it reached Jimmy's eyes, it stopped. At least it seemed to stop. He pulled the sheet over his face with a grunt and scrunched yet deeper into the world under his covers. Colors. Colors. He kept seeing colors rotating and even seething through screens only to become another shade of the same color. How could so few colors turn into so many more of such subtle feeling? A deep blue purple formed in his mind and pulsed, changing shape—oozing into new shapes, but always the bright color of indigo blue purple. Suddenly it displayed a brilliant yellow corona. Shoots of bright yellow bounced from the purple core into Jimmy's mind. The yellow turned to a deep orange, and the orange melted into red, and then to purple. A dance. For Jimmy alone. His own private special showing.

How many minutes or even eons went by in those moments? Time is simply a force that focuses eternity into three dimensions, allowing us to touch it, to smell it, to taste it. How nice of the universe to give us such patience—to slow itself down just so we can be a part of it.

The sun moved on its path around the curtain, the alarm went off, and Jimmy lost his purple friend and replaced it with beige socks. The memory filed itself under the sheet of his unconscious for a more appropriate time frame.

School came and went. He picked the good from it like one would pick apples off a large tree. He left the green ones and he left the rotten ones. He just picked the right ones for himself.

After school he lazily walked home. The sun was an autumn sun, still warm, but aloof. Each day was getting shorter, each night a little longer and a little colder. Fireplaces were starting to crackle with... Trees! Again TREES! Jimmy ran hysterically as though his friend were in peril. Trees! Oh, my God. Trees! NO NO NO, not trees! He was exhausted when he reached the apartment, and fell heavily onto the floor. Out like a light. Out like a thousand million hundred trillion lights. For what did it matter now that his trees were burning?

He slept soundly with no memory. Black was the only color in his mind. Deep black. The black of forgetfulness and escape.

The next sound clinked in his ear. Dishes. Someone was washing dishes. Not too loud, but loud enough to keep him from going back to sleep. The dishes kept clinking and obviously 'now' was when they were going to get washed. Oh Fate plays such mean little tricks sometimes.

"Jimmy, are you awake?"

"Uh," he forced out.

"Jimmy," she paused. "Are you upset about something?"

"I don't know, mom. Yes, I guess so."

"What's going on?"

How could he tell her he was upset about fireplaces. She was sure to think he was nuts.

"Nothing, mom. Nothing."

She left him alone. Any pushing now would have sent him deeper into his isolated prison. She was too smart for that, and he knew it.

He puttered for a while in his room and colored geometric designs with his pens. The designs were so perfect. And then the pens reminded him of his dreams about color. He started to watch them as he colored each form. How instinctively he picked up certain colors. He knew if he were blind, he would choose the same colored pens without hesitation. What was this thing about color? And how could color possibly be important except that it made things pretty?

Yet each time he picked up a pen, he knew he had chosen that particular color for a reason. A reason which was too far away to grasp. He colored and colored, and finally he felt better. Well enough to leave the safety of his room.

Good thing, too. Because dinner was ready. And it was spaghetti.

Chapter 11

A year ago Jimmy would have closed his eyes when they passed the garlic bread. Now he ate it with gusto. His problems seemed less important now that he was hungry and eating what he loved the most.

Onions, mushrooms, green pepper, garlic, hot sauce. He ate it all. How you felt about them was a definite indication of age.

"This is great, Mom," he spurted between the spaghetti strands. "I sure was hungry. Thanks."

It was already dark. The time had changed. That meant getting up was a little bit easier, but six o'clock seemed like bedtime. He felt better now. He even wondered how he could have gotten so upset. But he didn't dwell on why.

"I'm glad you're feeling better." She avoided asking him what was wrong. It would have been bad timing. "I really care about you, Jimmy. I feel your feelings sometimes just like they were my own. I can't help it, I guess. I know you better than anyone else in the world."

"Thanks." That felt good. He could feel her sometimes when she wasn't around, and he knew she was thinking about him. A warm feeling would come over him like a soft breeze in summer.

"Don't forget to change your guinea pigs' box tonight." She always turned practical after getting sentimental.

"I was going to."

He was lying, but it sounded good.

After dinner he dutifully changed his pigs' box. They were cute. But they sure did pee a lot. Every bottle of water turned into twice as much liquid in the box. But I guess they were worth it. He started thinking how funny they would look if he put them in diapers. He kept laughing as he formed their new cardboard home, and when he was finished, it looked like an apartment complex. Three boxes made twelve corners. Twelve corners instead of diapers. And he wouldn't have to deal with this chore for at least six days. Two corners per day—one corner per pig. It wasn't his favorite job, even though he loved the animals. The image of diapers kept making him laugh.

Chapter 12

"Hey, there, Jim!" Joel fumbled his keys back into his pocket and set down a horrendously heavy bag of groceries. "What's going on, you seem so glum lately."

"Oh, nothing."

"Well, I'll get you later. Hey, why don't you help me put these things in the refrigerator? Geez! What a mess this kitchen is. They've come up with self-cleaning ovens, please let them discover self-cleaning kitchens next."

"And self-cleaning bedrooms."

"And self-cleaning kids," his mother popped in.

"And self-cleaning cars..."

"Oh, stop! Enough!"

"Come on, mom, don't be a crab."

"Yeah, okay."

"And frost-free *winters*."

The temperature had dipped below zero again. Chicago had its ups and downs as far as weather. Up to over a hundred and down to well below zero. With the wind-chill factor, it probably was colder than the lowest temperature on Pluto. And spring was now just about as long as one rotation of the planet Earth. Lake Michigan had never been much of a Gulf of Mexico. And despite the influx of folk from farther south, San

Juan had to be some kind of paradise compared to this muck and ice.

And yet each snowstorm brought its delights. Snowflakes on your eyelashes. Millions and billions and trillions and a google of snowflakes in the air, on the ground, swirling overhead making you dizzy when you look at the sky. How wonderful.

"What do you want for dinner tonight? We can have spaghetti, homemade pizza, hamburgers, sloppy joes or peanut butter sandwiches."

"How about a peanut butter and banana pizza?"

A restaurant on North Clark, owned by a happy Greek man named Nick, made peanut butter and banana pizza. And other combinations. Pizzas that sounded *horrid* and actually tasted wonderful. And then Nick's restaurant burned down. What a pity—such a creative place it was. One night Jimmy had been standing at the counter admiring a set of Japanese coffee mugs. Nick pulled them out of the case. "L*ike* these?" He handed them to Jimmy. "They're yours." Not many people were that wonderful, not in Chicago, anyway, and Nick was. Nick was that wonderful. And so was his restaurant. And now it was burned. Maybe he was better off. Maybe he went back to Athens. No snow. Must be a nice place.

"Jim. Hey, Jim! Want to watch the football game with me?" It was Monday night. But it might have been Thursday. Monday night football on Thursday. Why didn't they just call it T*hursday* night football? He remembered all his confusion about why adults did things the way they did. Maybe when he grew up he'd know. But he doubted it. Adults were a different breed. When he grew up he wouldn't be adult.

"No, I don't think so. Maybe next Monday."

"Geez, Jimmy, that's NEXT WEEK!"

"Yeah, I know."

"What's going on with you, lately?" Joel went back into the TV room. Jimmy knew Joel didn't want to hear *why*. Not now. Jimmy went into his room and picked up "The National Lampoon".

He lay on his bed. "The National Lampoon" lay over his chest. His shoes were toppled at the foot of his bed, but he lay in full dress—jeans, socks, shirt. The works. His mother knew how it felt to wake up only to undress and go back to sleep, so she dimmed the light down to moonglow and left him to his dreams.

And they were potent this night.

He walked through a dense forest. Crying, sobbing for his trees that had been cut. Paper. Logs. Toothpicks. Newspapers. Oh God, why were all his trees dying? And worst of all fires. How could his beautiful trees end in flames? He trudged through thick vines filled with green leaves. In and out of fir trees soon to be cut for Christmas. He felt his limbs as branches reaching out to touch his friends. Limbs. Even in humans they called them limbs. Branching out. Taking root. The earth below, the sky as a never-ending goal.

But he couldn't forget his trees burning in each fireplace. Each specific fireplace. How many logs equal how many limbs times how many fireplaces?

the
magic of
FINDHORN

He slept with pain lingering over his heart. My trees, your trees, our trees. Oh please, let us have beautiful fires without hurting the trees.

His consciousness turned to dream. His dream became a universe. And in that universe was the answer to the pain he had been carrying for days. The answer was simple, as most important answers are. The trees that were burned had died long ago. It was their glory to burst into flame then dwindle into ember. The brightness. The last call. The beauty. The gift to man. The lovely symphony that plays itself in each hearth. That was a goal. The tree, no longer able to produce leaves and seeds, produced joy and warmth in each fireplace. In each home it entered.

Jimmy remembered the joy he received from each log lifted, each log burned. And then the joy seeped through his limbs. And he still felt his connection with the trees. The limbs of the trees with the limbs of his body. He slept a delicate sleep. A sleep he had needed for a long time.

13

It was Saturday. Saturday was always a wonderful morning. No school. Jimmy would jump up thinking he was late. Then sink back down into oblivion when he realized he didn't have to get up and rush around getting into his clothes. Saturdays were even better than Sundays because you knew you had *two* whole days before Monday started the 5-day chain. He could be lazy. He could be busy. He could be anything he wanted. No one would start out the morning by saying "Don't you think you..." That was usually followed by "ought". *Ought* was such a ridiculous word. It always means someone *else* is worried about what you *might not* do. Why didn't they trust that you had the intelligence to do what was necessary—when *you* felt like doing it?

But then, Jimmy's mom once said, "I have to keep changing as you change. Six months ago if I hadn't reminded you, you would have just forgotten. Not because you don't care. But when you start to do something, you get so involved, you just forget. It isn't wrong. But I never know when you move along in life until you get mad at me. And then I know I don't have to say that anymore. I need to grow as much as you do, and I'm really sorry if sometimes it sounds like I think you're stupid. I really don't. But you grow so fast, and I don't always know 'where you're at.'"

"Where you're at" was a phrase. It meant *who you are at the moment*. It meant the person didn't mean to bump into your feelings. And they really cared how you felt about things. "Lingo". That's what his mother called it. She said in 20 years it would be as out of date as "baby". No one would know what it meant. Like *cool, neat, far out*. But without "lingo" it wasn't as much fun to talk. "Knock yourself out." He could see the heavyweight champ hitting himself in the face, and started to laugh hysterically.

He had made a mistake. You can't laugh and stay in the land between wake and sleep. He scrunched around in the pillow and covers for a while trying to get back the magic feeling, and finally gave up.

He got up, stretched, and went into the bathroom. The feelings rushed through his body as he watched the bubbles. He remembered camping, and how much more fun it was to go on a tree. Well not exactly. At the bottom of the tree. He never could quite "pee" on a tree because of how he felt about trees. But he knew he could water the roots with what was in his body, and somehow that tree would turn it to good use.

He went into the kitchen and picked up the Heartland box, pulled the door of the refrigerator open, hoping there was milk. He reached for a bowl and spoon and began his morning ritual. The house was quiet. A nice time of the day. The cereal sounded loud as he chewed into it. The cold milk squeezed between the hard pieces of grain. One night they had a terrible storm and the electricity went out. It was fun at night with the candles because it felt so spooky. But in the morning the milk was warm. He started to think about how it must have been without electricity. Like being a cave man. That must have been a lot of work. No cereal in the morning. Crabby mothers who couldn't have a cup of coffee. Dads who hunted all day, and smelled bad at night because there were no showers or bathtubs. His mother would say, "Tonight we're having rabbit with roots." Yuk. Still, somehow, the thought haunted him.

Chapter 14

Jimmy had been feeling tense for days. But not from anything he could put his finger on. It was a feeling of something unresolved, something waiting to happen. He went about his daily life eating breakfast, going to school, watching "Star Trek", and generally enjoying himself. But something was happening.

It wasn't necessarily bad. Nor was it necessarily good.

The next morning his mom said, "Did you hear about the earthquake in Italy?" It wasn't really a question. It was more as though she were saying, "It's starting to happen. The earth is evolving, and one of these days it's going to start to happen faster and faster. And then, everything is going to change. Maybe too fast. But it's okay. Somehow everything is still okay."

Mount St. Helens had blown her top and was still rumbling. California was shaking at the top. Books on astrology were foretelling the Age of Aquarius. Even the possibility of a polar shift because of the planets aligning. Something different was happening. Maybe not as drastic as they were predicting, but something was happening. Jimmy sometimes saw all the trees on the planet holding it together. Pulling energy from the sky and putting it into the ground with their roots. Or taking the excess energy in the earth up through the roots and

putting it back into the sky. They didn't always take out enough so that's why there were volcanos. A bit far fetched. But not totally impossible. He didn't tell many people about this particular thought, however.

Math was going well in school. He had started algebra. Science was also exciting. They were starting to study astronomy of a sorts—junior high schools don't have very big telescopes. But now that it was getting darker earlier, he got to see the moon a few times through a modest telescope. That was so exciting! Mountains, craters, and so *close*. They all seemed so close. He wanted to walk through the telescope and slip down onto the surface, like a secret astronaut. But he didn't want to go by spacecraft in a suit. He wanted to just *be* there. Like a puff. In his secret fantasies this was possible.

English was not too boring lately. They had stopped diagramming sentences and were reading fiction. And now he had a new teacher. A new teacher for every subject—it was an "experiment" the school was trying to make it feel more like high school. Ms. Biedermann would never have gotten so excited about the moon as his science teacher, Joe Salazar. He didn't make you call him "Mr." Salazar. More and more often the kids were calling him "Joe." He was friendly and excited. And he was smart. So smart that Jimmy stopped looking out of the window and found himself squinting as he listened, leaning on his elbows with his chin solidly in his hands.

Joe was talking about black holes.

15

Gravity seemed to be the weakest of the four natural forces. Much weaker than electromagnetic or nuclear force. But when an object got really big, gravity was the most powerful of all.

Gravity, for Jimmy, used to be only something convenient when he played ball. Something inconvenient when he fell off his bike.

But now gravity was taking on a magnificence beyond all reason. Beyond what he had ever imagined possible. How could something so small as a large pearl comprise matter as great as the earth? Not that the earth would ever become a black hole, but how could something so big be condensed that much?

He listened with rapt attention each day in science class now, oblivious of time, ignoring the newly budding branches outside the window.

The bigger an object was, the greater the pull to its center. Atoms piled on atoms piled on more atoms. Each atom had a nucleus and at least one electron. The electrons kept the nuclei from touching, acting like a shell to keep the atom intact. Each (–) electron surface repelled each other (–) electron surface, the way two dog magnets did when they were backwards. That was electromagnetic force. So all the atoms pushing on each other toward the center of the earth by the force of gravity are being repelled by each tiny, negatively charged electron "shell". If they are piled too high, the shell caves in from the weight. Often the forces equal each other. Then everything stays intact. Squished, to be sure, like his tires were when he got on his bike. But not broken. That was the status of a planet. Gravity pushing inward; electron shells of atoms resisting. This caused stability. At least to the size of Jupiter. Maybe not there.

But what happened with something as big as a star? Like our sun, or a star a hundred times bigger than our sun? The gravitational pull on the surface of the sun is 28 times greater than on the surface of the earth. Enough to cave in atoms near the middle.

Jimmy thought of how it felt to be tackled on a football field with only a few other small bodies on top of him. He cringed at the thought of being an atom under all that smashing weight.

Crushing the electron "shells" did not destroy the electrons—it only freed them to move about unconstrained. Then, they were compressed more and more under the great weight in an unstructured form called "electronic fluid". His teacher called it "degenerate matter". The heavy part of the atom was its nucleus, and now all of these nuclei could get even tighter together under the packing forces of gravity. Yet, it was still electromagnetic force that was doing the pushing back.

And this was one of the differences between a star and a planet: at a critical point in size, it was too heavy

for the center to bear, and electromagnetic force was replaced by nuclear force in the fight for equilibrium. How big an object had to be before nuclear power was activated, no one knew. Somewhere between the size of Jupiter and our own sun.

In the sun, 80-90% of its atoms are hydrogen. Under such great gravitational pressures, these fuse to become helium atoms. The intense heat caused by the fusing atoms then does the pushing. As four hydrogen atoms fuse to form each helium atom, they're using themselves up, so to speak. So what happens when all the hydrogen atoms are fused up, or even when enough are gone so that the heat reduces?

The core would continue to compress from gravity, becoming hotter. The increased heat would cause the surface to expand. Because the surface took up more space, it would be cooler at the edges than it is now. It would be red and hot. Much cooler than white and hot. It would engulf Venus in its expansion, and be what his teacher called a "Red Giant".

Class was over and Jimmy walked through the budding trees smelling new spring flowers as he went home. Each day life seemed so much more interesting.

He decided to study tonight because it was hard for him to remember all the new names he was hearing, like "nucleon" and "positron".

Jimmy read for a long time. It was quite late. He didn't consider it studying because he was enjoying it so much. He was enjoying everything a lot nowadays. There were things to discover, and so many things to do.

Each day seemed like a new world. And in many ways it was just that.

He finally put the book down and slid over the rim of sleep. Now he was a cluster of neutrinos flying through the universe at the speed of light. The rushing sensation thrilled him. He—a massless particle flying through space with only joy to exude, only travel as a goal, flying as swiftly through matter as he did through the vacuum of black. Geometric forms populated the blackness of space. Outlines of bright green, red, purple, vermilion, and yellow. Each color of the spectrum blossomed into cubes and polyhedrons. He could see through some of them, as though they were mere skeletons of forms. Others glowed outwardly and changed shape, forming into groups and patterns, yet always keeping their single unit in perspective. He flew happily, and he laughed. Joy was like he knew it could be. He didn't stop to think of why or how he could perform such a feat. He just did it.

16

The sun peeked its head around the window frame. His covers had moved at night and a cold draught blew under one corner. He grabbed the edge of his blanket and rolled over until he was secure and cozy. He pulled his animal under his arm and nuzzled the pillow. Drifting off, he heard music far off in the distance. Not trying to figure out where it came from, he just enjoyed the pleasant moments before he had to brush his teeth.

The sun moved across Jimmy's window. Now in the morning, he knew his lazy time was over when the sun reached three-quarters the way to the other end of the window. He still had half of the window to go.

Nuzzling down into his pillow, he tried to go back to the dream he already forgot.

"Now, let's see. I felt like this. If I feel like this again, maybe I can get back there." He pushed and pushed at trying to feel like "this" again, but never made it. The slipperiness of dreams! What tricksters! It didn't matter if you wanted to remember—not if you woke up too fast. But when you only *halfway* woke up — then it MIGHT work. Someday he would learn to dream so well he could go back at will.

He sat daydreaming for a while, staring at the toilet paper roll. Then he focused on the soap dish over the bathtub. Then the towel. Then the rug. And then the stars. Somehow he could see the stars through all of the daily this-and-that. Time stopped. Perhaps he sat there for five minutes. But for Jimmy, he sat there just long enough to feel the stars forming his body universe—his fingers, toes, down his legs, in his brain. He could hear the stars and he felt they were singing to him.

"Hey, sweetie. You overslept. You'd better hurry, it's eight o'clock."

"Geez! You're kidding!"

Jimmy stormed out of the bathroom as if a bucket of ice water had hit him. Not because he was "late" but because he might be late for science. Socks whisked on tired sleeping feet, corraled by shoes. His shirt was sticking out from his pants.

"I'll brush my teeth when I get home," he wailed as he pounded down the front steps.

17

"What's gotten into him?" Joel poured a topper of coffee into his cup, bunched up his pillow and resumed reading his book. Eight fifteen was the magic hour for Joel, and he still had fifteen minutes to bask in his morning ritual.

Scrunching back under the covers, Jimmy's mom mumbled, "I think he's afraid he's going to be late for science."

"Looked more like he had a hot date."

"He did."

Jimmy ran down the sidewalk, but walked across the streets. An old message from his childhood told him never to run across streets. Then he fled down the next block, waved secretly to his tree, crossed the alley, under the viaduct, and soon was at school. Not terribly late, but his breathing sounded like a 747 and he was sure everybody was staring at him. Actually they weren't. After a mild coughing fit, he settled down to listening. He wasn't too late. He didn't miss it.

"...Even neutronium cannot hold up mass endlessly piled on mass. In 1939 Oppenheimer theorized that even neutrons will collapse and cave in to gravitational power. So what next? Oppenheimer decided there was no stopping point, for when nuclear power fails, nothing can stop gravitation—the weakest of all forces. The weight of all those atoms finally wins and beats down the walls of the neutronium."

Jimmy thought of all those little football figures and cringed. Surely it was more sophisticated than that, but it was good enough to understand the concept. Yet how could a star keep collapsing indefinitely, shrinking down to nothing in volume, yet its surface gravity increasing without limit? The mere thought boggled Jimmy's mind to its ends.

But then, his mind was probably like the universe and had no ends. He kept listening.

"As the surface gravity goes up, so does the escape velocity. Once the escape velocity gets beyond the speed of light, poof! You can't see it. It's as simple as that." Then he said something about a man called Schwarzschild, that Jimmy didn't quite understand.

"And that's why it's called a black hole. Even light can't get out."

Class was over again. Jimmy hung around for awhile. He finally went up to Joe.

"I really like what you're teaching us."

"I know. I can see it in your eyes when I talk. Here..." He pulled open his desk drawer and handed Jimmy a book. It was by Isaac Asimov, and it was called "The Collapsing Universe."

Jimmy ran home after school just as fast as he ran that morning.

18

As soon as Jimmy got home, he hardly could get the key in the door he was so excited. No one was home yet. He threw his books and jacket on the floor like he shouldn't, and screamed toward the bathroom. Why his key in the lock had such power, he never understood. But as soon as that key went in that little keyhole, his body went crazy until he could get through the door and to the john. He returned to pick up the rubble on the floor by the door. Set apart, as though by magic, lay his Isaac Asimov book. He forced himself to hang up his coat and put his books in a neat pile, then lifted "The Story of Black Holes" almost reverently, and went to his bedroom. He propped up his pillow and began paging through the book gently.

He read about gravity again. And electromagnetic force. How nuclear force was so much more powerful, but not after all was said and done. He read until he couldn't read any more. He dozed off, not knowing he was falling asleep.

He seemed to be floating in a mucky atmosphere, like being in a soup. At first he was frightened, but then he realized he could still breathe, so he just relaxed and enjoyed the oozing and bubbling. Then he seemed to lift somewhat and entered a clear crystalline element.

At the bottom of the pillars of crystal, he looked upward and saw colors arcing through the spectrum. He became a part of the crystal and then a part of each color, riding as if on waves, being each color instead of Jimmy. He was red. Then he was orange. He soared being purple. And all the while a majestic music — unlike any he had ever heard — filled his mind until he was laughing without laughter, crying without tears. For the first time in his life he knew why color existed.

Then he slept the sleep of the gods. And what is that? It's like the laughter of the gods.

It's without a reason. Just for itself.

19

A key clicked in the lock again. It was Jimmy's mom. She didn't seem to have the same problem Jimmy had with his key. At least not today.

She closed the door and felt his presence. But it was too early for him to be sleeping—yet the quietness of the house showed he was not about in any way.

She walked into the living room, then into his bedroom, and saw him askew on his bed, a new book over his chest, sound asleep. She watched him for a while then tiptoed out of the room.

In the kitchen again, she straightened the dishes before the chore of washing. Stacking plates of various sizes together, cups, glasses and silverware. It was too hard to cook with all the mess, and it became a sort of meditation for her to "make new" the daily mess that is so old, and re-turn a piece of chaos to a piece of order.

She began reminiscing about her father, who had died several years ago. She remembered as a child how she had nestled in his arms in his favorite chair. And painfully each Sunday the mirage would fade, and he would leave and go to his "new" family. Now, as an adult, she realized it was good that he had finally left an old relationship that had never worked and found happiness with another family. She remembered her own marriage—ill-fated, and how much pain "trying" to love was, when loving should be so simple. Why didn't people just let each other *be*? It was so easy. And now life itself was so easy because they, as a family, just "let each other be". They cared from the bottom of their hearts, but nobody tried to "control" the action. They just had fun together, and did their chores without fighting.

Jimmy wasn't the "kid" and she the "mom" and Joel the "dad". They called each other those names, but they knew they were *really* roommates. Not just plain old ordinary roommates, but roommates in Life. They were on the earth to teach each other beauty, joy, discipline, and truth. Truth wasn't THE truth. Truth was another part of joy. Truth without joy is not TRUTH. It just looks like it.

She stacked the forks and knives in a cup, and then washed each size plate in its turn. She enjoyed the compulsive stacking with some gambling to see how far she could go before a dangerously shaky pile was formed. That was the best part of doing the dishes.

Joel was late. She looked at the stove clock, then wiped the last counter clean.

Gratified, she went to her study to read.

She, too, dozed off, but went another place than where Jimmy was.

Chapter 20

Every afternoon when Jimmy got home from school the house was empty and quiet. Just right to read his new book. He had a favorite corner in the sun porch where he had pillows propped up. The afternoon sun left shadows of leaves on the walls, and when it was warm, he'd open the window and a breeze would blow gently through the room. He didn't read a lot each time. It was complicated. Some things he could understand, but some things he'd have to read over and over. Usually after two or three times he could understand the idea, but it was definitely an "adult" book. It took a lot of work sometimes, but he loved it. He liked noting where his bookmark was each time he picked up the book. It gave him a proud sense of accomplishment.

His teacher continued to teach about the universe and beyond. Many ideas Jimmy could see he took from Isaac Asimov. Yet that must have been what Isaac had intended. Joe always gave credit where credit was due, so he didn't act as if the ideas were all his.

The excitement of the class built with the mysteries of forces so powerful they were beyond his wildest

dreams. It made him know there must be *no limits to anything*. Not the universe. Not even to people. No limits to anything. That was so exciting to think about, Jimmy stopped putting limits on himself. He stopped thinking of himself as "little". He stopped putting limits on his brain, on his excitement, even on his love. He started liking his friends more. No. He started loving his friends more. He cared when something was bothering them. He got excited when *they* did, especially if they did something nice, or something good happened to them. He liked it when they went on vacation, or got good grades. He started seeing them through *their* eyes. Everything was more important now. Life was good. And he was almost a teenager.

He was thinking about light years one afternoon. The sun made patterns on the wall through the trees. He knew the sun was 93,000,000 miles away. It was still hot. He didn't know how long the light took to reach the earth. Did the heat travel at the speed of light, or at a different speed? Was the heat light? Then he started thinking about the stars, and remembered the phrase, "that star is 153 light years away", or "that star is 600 light years away". He started to think about light years. Suddenly he jumped up. "That means I'm seeing *now* 600 years in the past!" He got so excited he almost ran out of the apartment. He *could see the past*! The *past is now*! He must be in the *future* of the star! He was boggled by the idea that even time is not limited. He was seeing the past in the present. It was as though Jimmy had discovered it all by himself.

That night when he went to sleep, he *knew without thinking,* there were *no boundaries.* Not between now and the past, not between now and the future, not between himself and others. No boundaries.

The moon was particularly bright this night. He held his pillow tightly and felt the magnificence of life. And how glad he was to be a part of it.

21

Day began. Day. What is a Day? Routine. Brushing your teeth. Putting your socks on. Eating your cereal, after you've opened the refrigerator, taken out the milk, gotten a bowl, gotten a spoon, opened the cereal, dumped it in the bowl, closed the cereal and put it away (if you don't want to get hollered at). Pouring the milk, putting the milk away (if you don't want to get hollered at), and trying to eat it half asleep before it gets soggy.

But day meant more than that. Day meant Life. Day meant sunshine and fun. Laughter. Secrets. Seeing your new girlfriend. Running. Lunchtime. The park. Seeing a movie. Day had a lot of different personalities. Jimmy loved the day. And morning was the prelude to the Day. So he could tolerate the boring parts.

He finally found two socks that matched, a clean shirt and some pants that weren't too bad. He put it all together and looked fairly decent. By the time he combed his hair and brushed his teeth, he looked great.

He grabbed his books and tore out the door. "Bye! See you tonight!"

Running down the street felt good. He checked the stop light, cruised across the street, then ran, trying not to step on any lines in the sidewalk. After the rough winter he gave up lines and cracks and just concentrated on missing the lines.

School was interesting and it was fun being with his friends. He stayed late to stand on the corner and joke for a while. Then he went home feeling good. Feeling older.

The world was changing for Jimmy. As it was for everybody else. Most of the changes were fun. Some were a little uncomfortable, like learning to be with girls and feeling okay. Everything was exciting—getting up in the morning, the walk to school, passing his tree, meeting his friends. Girls especially were more fun. Last year they were boring. He was still excited about the universe, but he was interested in people, too. Why they were the way they were; what made them say the things they said; how much he liked them. And how much fun it was to laugh. Jimmy laughed a lot. He didn't play basketball or 'run'. He exercised his lungs and heart by laughing. Sometimes he would run home from school, but that was for fun, not for exercise. He wondered about all those people he saw that looked like robots jogging down the street. They never looked at people. They didn't laugh. He wondered what they did when they changed from their running shoes. What kind of shoes did they wear then?

22

He now said "Hi" to Ms. Biedermann in the hallways. She didn't seem so mean any more. He caught her smiling several times. Maybe she was happy in that special world she lived in. He cringed.

So many things had happened in his life, and more things happened each day. He never knew that time could hold so much. Even his sadness could be felt—if he saw someone crippled or terribly old having a hard time walking through the snow or carrying groceries, he helped them and sometimes cried later. Not a lot, but enough to make him feel the love for that person. He liked being twelve. It was the threshold of life. He remembered his childhood and he could sense his adulthood.

But what was it like to be an "adult"? His mother worked too hard. He knew that. Was that what it was to be an adult? But she laughed a lot and had friends who would go to the ends of the earth for her. Giving was a way of life with her, and little by little as Jimmy watched Joel and his mom, he knew what was really important about life.

The basketball game was important. But in a different way. It seemed to him that the most important thing in the whole wide world was love. And that meant laughter, hugs, being able to break someone else's treasure by accident, and they still loved you.

School was important. The stars were magnificently important. Trees. Flowers. Birds. And people. Everything was so important. Life brought him into her heart and held him all night long. He fell asleep with his pillow in his arms. And again he traveled to unknown lands that, by now, felt familiar.

Sometimes Jimmy wondered if other people experienced what he did. If they thought trees were like people, if they sometimes knew things were going to happen before they actually did happen, if when they were sleeping they could go other places while they lay in their beds, if they knew when someone was thinking about them or needing them. For some reason he never asked. He was afraid they might not, and then he would wonder if his experiences were "real"—and he didn't want to take that chance. He stayed away from mean people who hurt his feelings, and so was relatively safe from being laughed at. But even his very best friends only had a glimpse of who Jimmy really was.

Chapter 23

Time was passing swiftly.

He'd enrolled in high school. What had seemed like the end of the world was now just a beginning. In grade school, high school had seemed like an unattainable goal that he'd never reach. Now it was the beginning of a new stage of growth.

He didn't pass his tree anymore on his way to school, so on Saturdays he would walk there with a book, casually, just as though it were any other tree in the world, and he'd lean against it and read for hours until his butt started to itch from the damp ground. Then he'd lay his book down, get up, stretch, walk around the tree a few times, and if no one was looking, he'd lean against it and hug it. If he felt like reading some more, he'd lie on his side in the cool shade until his elbow hurt, and then he'd usually go home. Jimmy always felt the tree knew he was a friend—and that the tree knew when he was there. They had a friendship. Each did what each one had to do. But what he "had to do" was only a feeling, not a rule. They were partners. That he knew for sure.

Chapter 24

That night swirls of light filtered through Jimmy's mind. Purple descended with a radiance never known in light. Purple with the edges blackened by living ebony. Daylight with open eyes couldn't touch the beauty of this—only from the Mind could color become its own source.

Perhaps that's the field from which artists pluck their flowers.

And perhaps that's the field of light from which the spectrum was conceived. The Mother of Color.

Jimmy soared, floated, laughed, relaxed—the world of color embraced him. All else was second.

Only color was real.

The color of Night.

The color of the Universe.

The color of God.

The color of Jimmy.

Winter was over. The puddles in the street reflected new leaves on the trees. Saturdays held the special thrill of watching his favorite tree become new. The cycle of rebirth each Spring was an inspiration and a mystery to Jimmy, especially this year.

He knew they were moving, and he would be saying goodbye to this city that had brought him such joy.

Jimmy cried by his tree that Saturday. Oh, yes, they'd be there until summer, but the cord was cut. It was for certain they were leaving. The city rat race had become too desperate, and a new type of life was chosen by agreement. And it would mean separation. From his friends, from his school, from his beloved tree. The morning crispness turned his hot, salty tears into miniature rivers that streaked the sadness deeper into his face. Why did beginning something new always involve saying goodbye to something familiar? Why was there only so much room in decision making?

He had voted "yes" on moving, yet he was sore from the pain of parting with all he held dear.

He leaned his back against the cold trunk. It was uncomfortable and hurt. The familiar feelings were gone, as though the tree were pulling back in anticipation of being alone. Jimmy cried now without holding back. He leaned his forehead against his friend and sobbed his sadness dry. More love passed then between two species than the world could ever know.

The walk home felt empty.

His apartment home felt empty.

His lunch was tasteless.

Only pain was heavy in his body. Maybe he shouldn't move. But, then, he knew he must.

And he knew deep down he'd be happy again—some day.

That night Joel took Jimmy into the yard. They set up the telescope and aimed it at Jupiter and Saturn, which now were close to each other from our point of

view. You could see the rings of Saturn and the moons around Jupiter. The city lights blocked out a lot, and the noise of the nearby traffic took away some of the thrill.

"Jimmy, when we move, you'll see more stars by just looking up than you could ever dream of." Joel focused the scope, and then offered the eyepiece to Jimmy.

The mountains were waiting for them. Dry desert with sunsets of brilliant orange. Clouds and blue skies. Camping trips. Fishing. Star gazing. Skiing.

"Jimmy, I know you feel bad, and I'm sorry about that."

"Yeah."

"But I'll make you a promise. You see that?" He pointed to the heavens. "All that is yours."

He held Jimmy in his arms with the tenderness of a brother. The two stood there for a long time under the stars, and when they ended their embrace, the pain had left.

Jimmy knew love would fill the gaps he was sure to feel again.

And he thought of his stars, his quasars and his black holes as well as his tree.

Life held treasures beyond belief and he intended to discover them all.

The End